Quentin Blake

PATRICK

RED FOX

Some other books by Quentin Blake

All Join In
Angel Pavement
Angelo
Clown
Cockatoos
Fantastic Daisy Artichoke
The Green Ship
Loveykins
Mister Magnolia
Mrs Armitage and the Big Wave
Mrs Armitage on Wheels
Mrs Armitage Queen of the Road
Quentin Blake's ABC
A Sailing Boat in the Sky
Simpkin
Snuff
Zagazoo

PATRICK
A RED FOX BOOK 978 1 849 41665 8

First published in Great Britain by Jonathan Cape,
an imprint of Random House Children's Publishers UK
A Random House Group Company

Jonathan Cape edition published 1968
Red Fox edition published 2010

3 5 7 9 10 8 6 4

Red Fox Books are published by Random House Children's Publishers UK
61–63 Uxbridge Road, London W5 5SA

www.randomhousechildrens.co.uk

Addresses for companies within The Random House Group Limited can be found at:
www.randomhouse.co.uk/offices.htm

THE RANDOM HOUSE GROUP Limited Reg. No. 954009

A CIP catalogue record for this book is available from the British Library.

Printed in China

This is a story about a young man called Patrick,
who set out from his house one day to buy a violin.

Just then a girl and a boy came along the road.
Their names were Kath and Mick.

"Did you do that?" asked Mick, pointing to
the fish in the air. And Patrick said, "Yes."

Then he played another tune, and the string tying Kath's hair turned into red ribbons and the laces in Mick's boots turned into blue ribbons.

And so the three went down the road together. Soon they came to an orchard of apple trees. Patrick played his violin and the leaves on the trees changed to all kinds of bright colours.

Before long they met a tinker and his wife with a horse and cart.

"Look at our procession," shouted Kath. "Isn't it fun!"

"How can *he* enjoy it?" asked the tinker's wife. "He's very thin and I don't know what to do for him. He's got a cough and a cold and a stomach-ache and a headache. We have to travel so slowly, I don't know how we shall get to the town before dark."

"Let me play my violin and see what happens," said Patrick.

So he played a tune, and you can see what happened.

The tinker started to get fatter.